A
BEASTY
STORY

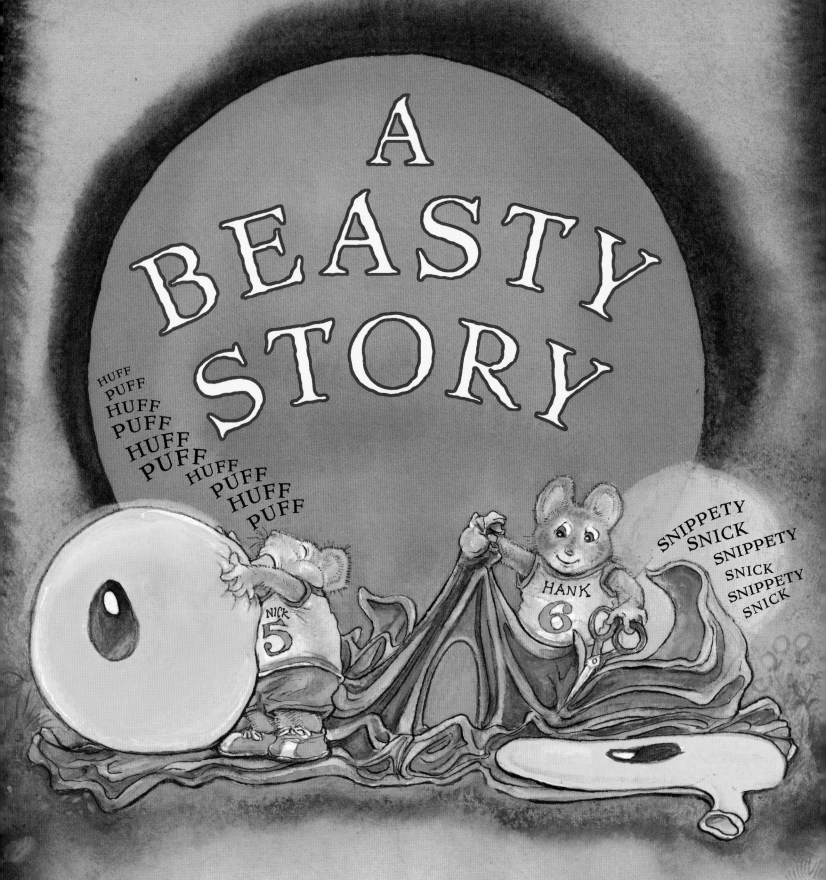

A BEASTY STORY

HUFF
PUFF
HUFF
PUFF
HUFF
PUFF
HUFF
PUFF
HUFF
PUFF

NICK
5

HANK
6

SNIPPETY
SNICK
SNIPPETY
SNICK
SNIPPETY
SNICK

Bill Martin Jr & Steven Kellogg

VOYAGER BOOKS · HARCOURT, INC.

San Diego   New York   London

www.HarcourtBooks.com

First Voyager Books edition 2002

Voyager Books is a trademark of Harcourt, Inc., registered in the United States of America and/or other jurisdictions.

The Library of Congress has cataloged the hardcover edition as follows: Martin, Bill, 1916–   A beasty story/by Bill Martin Jr and Steven Kellogg; illustrated by Steven Kellogg.   p. cm.

Summary: A group of mice venture into a dark, dark wood where they find a dark brown house with a dark red stair leading past other dark colors to a spooky surprise.

[1. Mice—Fiction. 2. Color—Fiction. 3. Stories in rhyme.] I. Kellogg, Steven, ill. II. Title.

PZ8.3.M3988Be 1999   [E]—dc21   97-49519   ISBN 0-15-201683-X   ISBN 0-15-216560-6 pb

E F G H

With love and appreciation
to Michael Sampson and his family
—B. M. & S. K.

In a dark, dark wood
there is a dark, dark house.

In the dark brown house
there is a dark, dark stair.

there is a dark, dark cellar.

there is a dark, dark cupboard.

there is a dark, dark bottle.

There is something inside

the dark green bottle.

A BEAST!

It floats out of the dark green bottle,

through the dark purple cupboard,

up the dark red stair,

into the dark, dark night,

through the dark, dark wood,

toward an even **DARKER** house,

into a dark orange room,

and GRABS HIM!

There is a flash of light!

sounds of beasty laughter,

The first collaboration between two beloved creators of children's books!

BILL MARTIN JR is known worldwide for his classic picture books, including *Brown Bear, Brown Bear, What Do You See?* and *Polar Bear, Polar Bear, What Do You Hear?*, both illustrated by Eric Carle, and *Chicka Chicka Boom Boom*, illustrated by Lois Ehlert. Mr. Martin lives in Texas.

STEVEN KELLOGG has illustrated more than a hundred dearly loved books for children, including *A Hunting We Will Go!* and his own versions of the ever-popular tall tales *Johnny Appleseed*, *Pecos Bill*, and *Paul Bunyan*. Mr. Kellogg lives in Connecticut.